Let's Hear It For
Bulldogs

Written by

Piper Welsh

Scan for Related Titles
and Teacher Resources

www.rourkeeducationalmedia.com

PHOTO CREDITS: Cover, Page 6, 7, 9, 16: © Tetiana Katsai; Page 4: © AP Images, Scott A. Miller; Page 5, 14: © MilsiArt; ; Page 8: © digihelion; Page 10: © Kit Sen Chin; Page 11: © Imagesbybarbara; Page 12: © Waldemar Dabrowski, John_ Woodcock; Page 13: © Peter Bokhorst; Page 14: © trebuchet; Page 15: © Al Braunworth; Page 17: © Yulia Popkova; Page 18: © onetouchspark; Page 19: © iofoto; Page 20: © John McAllister; Page 21: © cynoclub; Page 22: ©Eric IsselÃƒÂ©e

Edited by: Precious McKenzie

Cover design by: Renee Brady
Interior design by: Ashley Morgan

Library of Congress PCN Data

Welsh, Piper.
  Let's Hear It For Bulldogs / Piper Welsh.
    p. cm. -- (Dog Applause)
  Includes index.
  ISBN 978-1-62169-866-1 (hardcover)
  ISBN 978-1-62169-761-9 (softcover)
  ISBN 978-1-62169-967-5 (e-Book)
Library of Congress Control Number: 2013936477

Rourke Educational Media
Printed in the United States of America,
North Mankato, Minnesota

rourkeeducationalmedia.com

customerservice@rourkeeducationalmedia.com • PO Box 643328 Vero Beach, Florida 32964

Table of Contents

For over fifty years, the University of Georgia has had a white Bulldog as their mascot.

English Bulldogs

The English Bulldog's reputation for toughness and its wide, wrinkled face are famous. Who does not recognize those jaws and **jowls**?

Did you know that many schools have adopted the Bulldog as their mascot? And, a diesel locomotive is called "bulldog" because of its broad, blunt front. But are Bulldogs really the tough guys they appear to be?

Bulldog Facts

Weight:	40-60 pounds (18-27 kg)
Height:	12-15 inches (31-38 centimeters)
Country of Origin:	England
Life Span:	8-10 years

The first English Bulldogs were strong, vicious dogs. They fought bulls in pits. Modern Bulldogs look much like their ancestors, but they are not vicious. Instead, they are gentle, loveable companions. They are among the most mild-mannered dog **breeds**.

Most Bulldogs are sweet and playful pups who do well with families.

Those wrinkles are adorable but they require special care
to prevent bacteria from growing and causing an infection.
Most Bulldog owners use baby wipes to clean between
the wrinkles.

Look at Me!

A Bulldog stands on short legs, it is just 12 to 15 inches (30.5 – 38 centimeters) tall. Its head and shoulders are large. It carries much of its weight in the forward part of its body, like a miniature bison.

Male Bulldogs are usually heavier than female Bulldogs and look more bullish than the females.

Bulldogs are notorious for bad breath. Regular teeth cleaning is a must.

Bulldogs have small, floppy ears and naturally short, sometimes curly, tails.

To describe the shape of the Bulldog's ears, breeders say the ears are rosed.

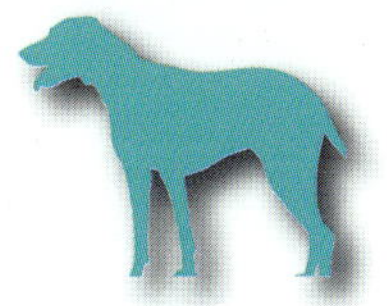

Bulldogs can be all white or have reddish, fawn-colored, or black markings on a white background. Some have faint striping in a pattern called **brindle**.

This Bulldog has a brindle pattern and the classic bullish look of the breed.

History of the Bulldog

We know little about the early ancestors of the Bulldog. Some believe that the breed developed largely from **mastiffs** and terriers in England.

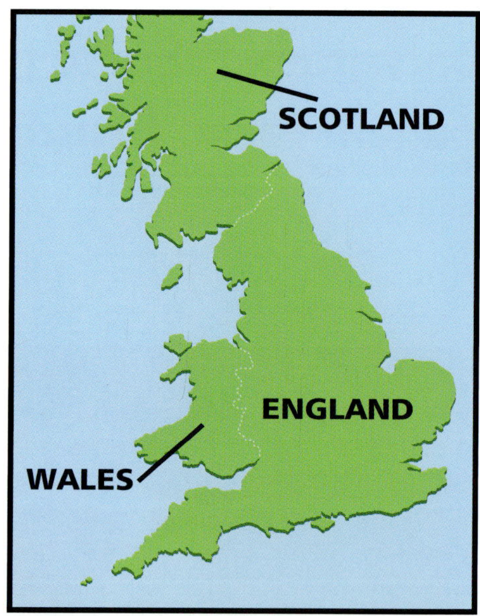

Mastiffs are thought to be ancestors of the Bulldogs because they share the same large, floppy jowls and sour facial expression.

The modern Bulldog is not naturally vicious and would rather be a companion than a fighter.

As bull **baiters** long ago, fearless Bulldogs bit onto the noses of tied-up bulls. Many people believed that a bull's meat would taste better if the animal was first bloodied in a fight. Bull baiting in England became a sport for spectators and dog owners. They also watched bears fight Bulldogs.

Bulldog Facts

Today, in the United States, any form of animal fighting is illegal.

Like all dogs, Bulldogs enjoy chewing. It is a good idea for Bulldog owners to have plenty of chew toys.

England stopped bull fighting in 1835. Now the main reason to raise Bulldogs was gone. The Bulldog breed began to disappear.

A few Bulldog **breeders**, however, wanted to save the Bulldog breed. Over the years, they chose less **aggressive** Bulldogs to be parents. The result of their careful work is today's good-natured companion dog.

Early training and socialization makes Bulldog puppies into wonderful pets.

A Loyal Companion

Bulldogs, wrinkles and all, are difficult not to like. They even greet strangers good-naturedly. They love attention and wag their tails, what little they have to wag, with great energy. A guard dog the Bulldog is not.

Because of the Bulldog's shape and size, puppy litters tend to be small. The average litter is usually three to five puppies.

If you are looking for a laid back companion, not a high performance athlete, a Bulldog might be a good choice for you.

Bulldogs need outdoor exercise, but not a great deal of exercise. They are neither distance runners nor swimmers.

Many Bulldogs can earn basic **agility**, tracking, or obedience titles. But Bulldogs are more indoor than outdoor companions. They would like to be lap dogs, but the average Bulldog weighs about 50 pounds (23 kilograms). That is more dog than most owners want on their laps!

Bulldogs have short coats, so they do not need constant brushing. Bulldog wrinkles require regular care so that they remain clean and free from infection.

All of the varieties of Bulldogs are adorable. With proper training and socialization, Bulldogs make wonderful pets.

Bulldogs need little brushing, unlike long haired dogs, such as Shih Tzus, that require almost daily grooming.

Bulldogs do participate in agility trials but Bulldogs are not as athletic as some of the working breeds.

Doggie Advice

Puppies are cute and cuddly, but only after serious thought should anybody buy one. Puppies, after all, grow up. Remember, a dog will  require more than love and patience. It will need healthy food, exercise, grooming, medical care, and a warm, safe place to live.

A dog can be your best friend, but you need to be its best friend, too.

Choosing the right breed for you requires homework. For more information about buying and owning a dog, contact the American Kennel Club at *www.akc.org/index.cfm* or the Canadian Kennel Club at *www.ckc.ca*.

Glossary

aggressive (uh-GRESS-siv): wanting to attack or attacking

agility (uh-JILL-uh-tee): the ability to perform certain athletic tasks, such as leaping through a hoop

baiters (BAYT-erz): animals used by people to anger another animal into attacking it

breeds (BREEDS): particular kinds of domestic animals within a larger, closely related group such as the English Bulldog breed within the dog group

breeders (BREE-duhrz): people who keep adult dogs and raise their pups especially ones who does so regularly and with great care

brindle (BRIN-duhl): a pattern in which vertical lines show in an animal's coat

jowls (JOULZ): loose flesh about the cheeks and lower jaws

mastiffs (MASS-tifs): any one of several breeds of very large dogs with that name

Index

Websites to Visit

www.akc.org/breeds/bulldog

www.dogbreedinfo.com/bulldog.htm

www.bulldogsworld.com

Show What You Know

1. How much does the average adult Bulldog weigh?
2. What are two things Bulldogs can't do?
3. What is the average life span of a Bulldog?